Rabbits & Dinosaurs

Preethi

Ukiyoto Publishing

All global publishing rights are held by

Ukiyoto Publishing

Published in 2023

Content Copyright © Preethi

ISBN 9789360164904

All rights reserved.
No part of this publication may be reproduced, transmitted, or stored in a retrieval system, in any form by any means, electronic, mechanical, photocopying, recording or otherwise, without the prior permission of the publisher.

The moral rights of the author have been asserted.

This is a work of fiction. Names, characters, businesses, places, events, locales, and incidents are either the products of the author's imagination or used in a fictitious manner. Any resemblance to actual persons, living or dead, or actual events is purely coincidental.

This book is sold subject to the condition that it shall not by way of trade or otherwise, be lent, resold, hired out or otherwise circulated, without the publisher's prior consent, in any form of binding or cover other than that in which it is published.

This title is produced in Association with Pachyderm Tales

www.pachydermtales.com

ACKNOWLEDGEMENT

I whole heartedly thank,

Mohanasundari Jaganathan,

(Managing Director of Sharp Electrodes Pvt Ltd)

for funding this project.

Without her, this book would not be possible!

This book was a part of workshop conducted in our college, NGM College Pollachi and Pachyderm Tales.

I whole heartedly thank our management, our teachers and HOD of English Dept, NGM as well as Suja Mam for this initiative.

Once upon a time, there was a beautiful forest which was the home to many animals and trees.

A small rabbit family was living a lovely life in the huge forest.

Their little family consisted of
the father rabbit, Kubbre,
the mother rabbit,
Mini and
their cute and chubby son, Chichu.

His father was strict, like a military man. The mother Mini, however, was loving and caring, and Chichu was always mischievous with her.

One evening, Kubbre and Mini went out in search of food and they asked Chichu to not leave the house.

In the end, Chichu thought that searching for food would be helpful for his parents, so he headed out. When he saw some carrots, he ate them happily.

After sometime, as he was going deep in to the thick forest, he forgot his way back home and was stuck in the middle of the forest. He became scared and moved forward.

Then he saw a big dinosaur cave and he went inside out of curiosity. The cave was dark that Chichu could not figure out anything.

In the corner of the cave, he saw something like a white ball.

He went near to it and touched it softly, but it suddenly fell down. It was then that Chichu realized that it was a large egg.

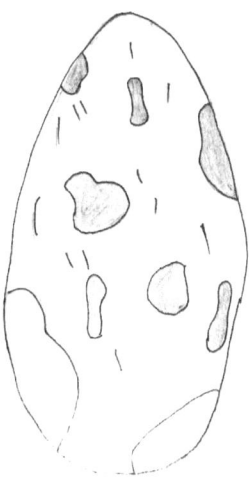

Chichu went around the egg, examining. But unfortunately, the cracking sound disturbed the mother dinosaur from her sleep.
Her name was Darksmoke.

The huge giant like dinosaur came near Chichu. Her face was furious with anger. Poor Chichu was awestruck. He didn't know what to do.

The mother dinosaur suddenly stopped, as the egg fully cracked and a pretty little dinosaur came out of the egg.

Darksmoke was excited to see her baby and they cuddled each other, licking on each other's faces. She named the baby dinosaur Kiwi.

After seeing all the love, Chichu remembered his family and started crying. He asked Darksmoke to help him to find his house and parents.

Darksmoke consoled Chichu and convinced him that they would find his family the next morning as it was dark by then.

The next morning, they all woke up with the mission to find Chichu's home and family.

Chichu and Kiwi were starving and they decided to go in search of some food first.

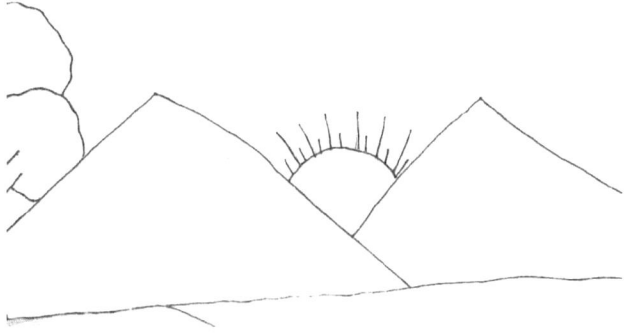

They went out of the cave and dived in to the forest and got lots of fruits and berries and ate them all.

As they went past the trees and mountains, they came across a stream flowing from the mountain top.

They loved the scene and decided to stop there for some time.

As they sat on the banks and splattered water on each other's face, Chichu and Kiwi slipped into the deep stream which was overflowing with water.

Darksmoke was frightened by the scene and jumped inside the stream to save them.

With a lot of struggle, Darksmoke managed to save Kiwi and Chichu.

In a rush to help the both, the mother herself lost her balance and slipped in to the water and started drowning.

The poor little Kiwi and Chichu could not do anything other than shout for help. They took all their strengths and started shouting and crying out loud.

After a while, Kubbre, the father rabbit, and Mini, the mother rabbit, who were in search of their lost son, heard the loud cries and gathered near the stream.

They were very excited and happy to see Chichu again.

They could feel the distress on Chichu's and Kiwi's faces and inquired about the situation. Chichu narrated all that happened after he left his home.

Kubbre and Mini were so glad to help Darksmoke and rescued her from the stream. She was unconscious by then.

Kubbre and Mini took Kiwi with them, along with Chichu, to their place and convinced her to stay with them until Darksmoke came.

After a week, Darksmoke regained her consciousness and she searched for Kiwi all around. She couldn't find Kiwi nearby and was sure that she would be there with Chichu and family.

She went in search of the rabbit house and spotted one after a long walk.

 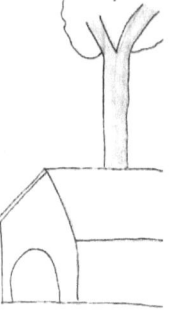

Just as she thought, Kiwi was staying with the rabbit family. The rabbits were very happy to meet Darksmoke in her full health once again and welcomed her.

She saw Kiwi playing with Chichu inside the house and cuddled her for a long time.

Darksmoke thanked Kubbre and Mini and she kissed Chichu. They all became good friends forever.

The Author

The story 'Rabbits and Dinosaurs' is the first published book by Preethi, who is a third-year English literature student at NGM College. She is an innovative artist, writer, and illustrator. Her goal is to spread happiness, love, and hope to everyone through her book. Her passion for family, friendship, writing, and photography fuels her passion for pursuing her dreams.

www.ingramcontent.com/pod-product-compliance
Lightning Source LLC
LaVergne TN
LVHW041601070526
838199LV00046B/2085